WHISPERS OF PACHAMAMA

A NOVELLA

Lucía Ashta

Awaken to Peace Press
SEDONA, ARIZONA

Awaken to Peace Press
Sedona, Arizona
United States of America
www.awakentopeace.com

This is a work of fiction. Names, characters, places, and incidents are a product of the author's imagination. Any resemblance to actual people, living or dead, or to businesses, companies, events, institutions, or locales is completely coincidental.

Special discounts are available on quantity purchases. For details, contact the publisher.

Whispers of Pachamama / Lucía Ashta -- 1st ed.
ISBN 978-0-9832743-1-5

Discover more of Lucía's work at www.luciaashta.com.

Dedicated to Mother Earth, mother to us all

When your eyes cannot see,
your heart can guide you,
for it is always true.

CHAPTER ONE

A Flickering Vision of Browns

WHEN the final moments of life arrived, he wondered how he had missed the signs, the clues to who she was. It was unbearable to think that he had not realized, that his blindness could have hurt her. There must have been something that he didn't see, but could have seen, that would have revealed the true nature of the woman he loved before the bitter moments of hindsight arrived with the crystalline clarity of death.

He might not have known who she was, yet he couldn't tear his eyes from her since the moment he first caught a glimpse of her, flashing like a fragmented picture among the thick trees of the jungle. He wasn't usually alone in the forest. It was dangerous. Deep in the heart of the Amazon, creatures that looked like they belonged to the races of mythical beasts were everywhere.

Raised in one of the small towns that edged the rainforest, he had learned long ago that just because you didn't notice a threat, didn't mean there wasn't one.

Everything in the Amazon was larger than life. Creatures and plants were bigger than it seemed they should be and infinitely more colorful than appeared necessary. The forest was never silent. Sounds echoed and mimicked one another, never ceasing.

He was normally careful to take his breaks with one of his fellow workers. They too were from the neighboring town, a town built to house loggers. There was no other reason for the village to be there. It was too remote to feel like much of a village at all, removed from the rest of civilization, and dangerous because of its proximity to the jungle. Everyone from that settlement—loggers, fathers and mothers of loggers, sons and daughters of loggers—was wary of the jungle's sprawling life.

Yet now, he didn't know where the others had gone—strange—and he was too tired to wait for them even though he knew he should. It might have been wiser to go look for them, but he would risk getting lost. He knew the jungle as well as his companions. Still, anyone could get disoriented. The forest was dense with growth, and it looked virtually the same in all directions—except for where they had cut down the trees.

But today they weren't cutting. They were surveying where to commence the next day. They had logged the other side of the jungle closest to Guayucuma, leaving a vast clearing around their town, which made the villagers feel safer now that they could see open ground.

It was time to expand into another section of the thick jungle, once they decided where it would be easiest to begin. In some areas of the forest, the vines and undergrowth wrapped around the trees so densely as to make their jobs several times harder. There were no parts of the forest that weren't like this, thick with life everywhere, but there were some that were a bit less so.

They were out there searching for the a-bit-less-so today. When he stopped, tired from trampling through the forest, slashing left and right with a machete, he was the only one there to see the woman.

He didn't know if he would have noticed her if he'd still been moving. Getting through the jungle was strenuous work. And his eyes constantly roved the forest floor and tree canopies. Things—poisonous things— hung or lingered everywhere in perfect camouflage.

It wasn't when his eyes swung methodically down, forward, left, right, upward, and then back down again that he saw her. It was when he stilled and wasn't really looking for or at anything in particular.

He was holding his scarred thermos to his lips when she flashed by. He sprung to standing and spilled hot yerba mate on himself. He shook the liquid off, never looking down.

With sharp eyes, he trailed her path. He couldn't see her anymore. Yet she had been right there.

What was a woman doing in the rainforest? He took a step toward the old, gnarled trees she'd just passed, but stopped, relying on his eyes to explore instead. His path was blocked by hanging plants that clung to tree branches, as thick as the thighs of giants. He would almost certainly lose her if he tried to rip through to her. He feared he might have already lost her.

He forced himself into total stillness. He was even quieter than the plants that grew one nearly indiscernible stretch at a time. Even his heart paused in its beating while he searched the tapestry of the Amazon for what shouldn't have been. He knew everyone from Guayucuma, which wasn't hard when there were so few. No one would be out here alone, especially not a woman.

Once an old woman had gone crazy. She had been one of those that came from the bigger city to escape its overpopulation. She began talking of the spirits of the forest and how the villagers needed to show them respect, and took her mad ranting into the jungle to leave it there. She disappeared one day and didn't return.

Her family didn't find her body. Anacondas could swallow a human whole.

That had been a long time ago. When she vanished he had been a young boy, too young to realize what had happened. He heard the story later.

No one had wandered into the jungle alone since then, neither man nor woman.

Now, he did.

There she was again. His heart resumed its pumping, racing loudly in his eardrums.

She had appeared on the other side, a blur concealed by eager trees. Then she faded into the woven fabric of the Amazon, swallowed whole as if sharing the same fate of the crazy, old woman.

He took one step toward her, or where she had previously been. He hesitated. The old woman hadn't been the only villager to die, a fate that the jungle freely handed out.

Then he spotted her again, farther away this time, whipping through the overgrowth impossibly fast, like an animal. No human could navigate the wilderness the way she did.

His feet began to move, and he didn't stop them.

With his machete out, it took him a long time to reach the spot where he'd most recently seen her. He feared she wouldn't be there anymore. She could be anywhere by now, even returned to wherever she had come from, and it wasn't Guayucuma.

Like a miracle, there she was. Not where he last noticed her, but close by, within view of the river. From there she moved slowly, cautiously, as if she finally realized the dangers that encircled her. She must have sensed him there, looking at her, but she didn't do anything to indicate that she had.

Unconcerned by her nakedness as much as she was by her surroundings, she walked toward the huge, wild river as if every place she stepped had been waiting for her to touch it. She traversed the distance between her and the river with a gracefulness and purpose he had only witnessed in the animals of the forest. Animals had been designed perfectly—nothing was out of place; nothing was superfluous or lacking—and they moved as if they knew it.

Her body was round and voluptuous in places, strong and limber in others. Long, thick black hair trailed over the brown skin of her back, swinging with each of her movements. He thought then that he would like to follow her anywhere, and moved closer.

As he was able to make out more of her features, he forgot that he'd meant to warn her of the dangers—as if, somehow, she just didn't know of them. He forgot about everything but this vision before him.

He offered all of himself to her even though she hadn't asked for it—she hadn't even looked back at him. When it became evident that she meant to enter the water, he fumbled through the last few steps to reach her, thrashing inelegantly at the plants that impeded his way, hacking at them until they relented.

"Wait." He didn't know if she spoke his language. The founders of Guayucuma had brought the Portuguese of the big city with them, but the natives of the area didn't speak it. They had their own language that only they and the plants and the animals understood.

She stopped and waited, but she didn't turn.

"You cannot go into the water."

She extended a long, brown leg toward it. Her calf muscle arched while she dipped the tip of her big toe into the river. "Why can I not go into the water?" She spoke Portuguese to him though the rhythms of her voice were different, somehow even more lyrical than his own melodic Portuguese.

He took one more step toward her and sheathed his machete on his belt. "Because it is very dangerous. Many creatures that live in this water can hurt you."

He didn't dare to move closer to her; she still hadn't faced him. His eyes trailed her body, down to the bare feet, which seemed impervious to the perils that rose from the fertile dirt of the Amazon. He would have averted his eyes to respect her modesty if she hadn't seemed so comfortable with her nudity. And it was difficult for him to resist the allure of a body with perfect hills and valleys.

"The water will not hurt me, nor will any creature within it." She dipped her entire foot into the river, and he became frantic. No one in his village risked entering this water. They built wells for their needs. He couldn't bear to watch the river, with all its caimans, anacondas, and carnivorous fish, eat up this woman.

He lunged for her arm and turned her toward him. It was only then that she met his eyes. Hers were a rich brown that looked as warm as her skin, soaked with sunshine, felt to his touch.

He froze in her stare, knowing he should withdraw his hand from her, but seemingly unable to move. All his intended words that would further warn and convince her to spare herself from death by suicide—because that's what stepping into the Amazon River was—vanished.

"You do not trust Nature." Slowly, slower than anything he had seen her do, she lowered her eyes to the hand that still clenched her bicep. Just as slowly, he released her. "I do."

She turned to the water, and put her muddy toe back in. She smiled, but only to herself; he could see just half of it from over her shoulder. Then, she walked into the water up to her knees. Next went her round hips. Then she waded in up to her waist, where the tips of her black hair touched the water and connected to it, urging her further in.

Another step, and her breasts floated atop the water, bobbing with the current. Down to her neck, and he couldn't bear it any longer. It would be any moment now that the piranhas would tear her beautiful flesh from its bones. He looked away for a second—but who was he kidding, he couldn't look away from her—and then she went completely under, a trail of black hair left floating on the surface like the veil of mourning for the loss of a life.

He waited for death to come and rip the miracle from him, a miracle whose name he had not learned. But death, usually overly punctual, didn't come. Her hair saturated and sank, unhurriedly.

She swam across the width of the river, and yet death didn't keep its appointment. She emerged onto the opposite shore, her calves coated in the silt of the soft riverbank. There, she did turn to look at him with those unchanged brown eyes that were of a richer color than any he had ever observed. How could he have never seen that shade of brown before? He spent most of his life in a forest full of browns.

She turned and took that deep, multi-dimensional brown with her. Then, without further acknowledgment, she walked into the jungle. Before long, the sparse foliage of the riverbank gave way to thick overgrowth.

She disappeared from whence she came, knowing that he would never follow across the river.

CHAPTER TWO

The Futile Search for Confirmation

MONTHS passed. They were long, quiet months split between the man's time logging and his time recovering from the effort. He had begun to wonder whether the woman in the forest was a product of his imagination. Perhaps his life was so monotonous—every day looked much the same as the one before it—that he had actually made the woman up as a diversion, his mind desperate for something different. And if it had to be something different, why not a beautiful, alluring woman? It was exactly the kind of thing his imagination would dream up.

The others believed him, the others that he'd told. There weren't many to whom he'd confided the encounter directly, but the village was small. The story spread, causing varying reactions among the people. Some thought the woman was a mythical creature of the forest. They suggested that she was a messenger or a savior sent to help them, though all they needed saving from was themselves.

Others considered her a bad omen. Maybe she was flesh and blood, and maybe she wasn't, but her arrival couldn't be a good sign. What kind of naked woman would walk into the Amazon River and submerge in its waters? None they wanted to encounter. No one that didn't have supernatural powers would swim in the Amazon like that, and the townspeople didn't like unexplained supernatural powers.

Others still argued that she was from another village—even though there was none near—and that she was lost—although she didn't seem lost. The fact that she was naked and swimming in the Amazon River just showed how much she needed their help. They had to save her before the jungle devoured her, if it hadn't already.

There were even a few more theories with a lesser following that sprouted up intermittently across Guayucuma. There was little else to distract them from the humdrum of their lives. They clung to what was already becoming a legend.

The man found it interesting that everyone had a theory or a version of the story that slightly deviated from his own, yet not one of them questioned what he'd

said. It was only he who wondered whether he had finally gone mad like the crone that disappeared into the jungle to her death.

He relived every moment of seeing the woman, over
and again, as vividly as if each were a hallucination, each
time questioning if she could have been real. She had
seemed tangible then, but the more he mulled over how
she looked and how she moved, the more he perceived
an unreal element about her that he had been too captivated before to notice.

He longed desperately to see her again, to prove himself either sane or insane, but to know at least which of
the two he was. But mostly he longed to see her again
because he ached with the desire to be near her, to be
close to that extraordinariness that she possessed, and to
share in her trust of the rainforest. He had feared the
jungle all his life, since he was old enough to understand
the villagers' warnings of the perils it shrouded, in every
possible crevice.

Observing her, he had not been afraid. He wasn't certain what he had felt for this unknown woman, but he
recognized that he had experienced something new,
something contrary to the usual hollow feeling of routine and survival.

With her, it was about more than survival, so much
more. And he wanted desperately to ascertain what that
was.

But as much as he searched for her, looking in the same places she had been and also in others, she eluded him. There was not so much as a broken glimpse of her among stout trees. So he kept cutting them down as he was supposed to, hoping that she could still show up when all the trees that concealed and revealed her to him were gone.

CHAPTER THREE

The Jungle Welcomes Its Own

EVENTUALLY, she did reappear, but almost half a year had gone by in the world of men, time never to be recovered. The man had given up hope and concluded that he had to be crazy, even though no one else in Guayucuma believed him so.

He attempted to understand the nature of his madness, but instead, he glimpsed his first real understanding of the nature that surrounded him. Raised in fear of his environs, he had never speculated about what lay past the danger. His thoughts had always been of caution, of what could be lost, and what must be saved at all costs.

But on that particular day he noticed more about the jungle. He looked all around him and saw the abundant life for what it was instead of the many ways that it could harm him.

For the first time since he spotted the woman running amid trees, he was alone again, out in the middle of nowhere, where he spent half of his days. He was part of a team of four. Two of the other men were around his age, still young and able to withstand the wear of muscle and bone that their work demanded without much more than regular soreness that went away, or mostly went away, by the next morning.

The fourth man was quite a bit older. Although not really old, he looked worn out by the hard work of earning his living. But he was tough as their gas-driven chain saws, and often the last one going, taking down one final tree toward their monthly quota of logs for shipment to the big city before they called the day over.

Once again, when the man stopped to wipe the sweat from his brow with the back of his slick hand, he noticed his three work companions—even the weathered man that could outdo them all—gone, vanished. That was what had happened last time, the time he saw the woman.

The man sat down on a fresh tree stump, and for once, he hoped his coworkers would take a long break. He plunked his chainsaw down with too little care, as if it weren't the device that dealt death to the jungle all day long.

His shoulder muscles ached. It felt as if his arms were still vibrating with the saw as it sliced. He would probably still be able to feel the shaking in his arms when he was dead. Sometimes, he would wake up from sleep to the muscles in his arms twitching, after the long hours of holding that blasted saw.

With calloused fingers, he tipped his ceramic vessel to his mouth. It was one the aboriginal tribes in the area made, brown like the dirt, a remnant from an old trade route that the natives were no longer interested in keeping. The villagers of Guayucuma had little to offer the indigenous tribes, who knew the jungle so well that they could find anything they needed within it.

The water felt cool on his tongue, though he couldn't be certain it was actually cool. Maybe it was just because he was so damned hot. He was always hot. Somewhere around six months had passed since he'd seen the woman, yet the seasons had not changed. Seasons never changed in the Amazon. He had only experienced one season his whole life, and that season was hot and humid.

He sat in the shade of the tree he would cut down next and wondered whether he should pour water over his head. He never had before, not while he was still out in the jungle. If he ran out of water, he might feel desperate with thirst (though it had never happened), and he didn't dare drink from any of the water that ran unconcernedly around him.

That got him thinking about the woman and how she had slipped into the Amazon River. She, or the imaginings of his mind, was incredibly daring.

Yet, what if the river wasn't as dangerous as he believed? What if his attitude toward the river made a difference? The woman had said that she trusted nature, and that he didn't.

It was then that he saw her again. He let go of these thoughts, so foreign to him, along with the worry of what might come, and lost them to the river.

He let go of anything but her. He clunked his earthenware vessel to the ground without care to reach toward her with desperation.

Yet he didn't move a muscle.

He waited. Only his gaze followed her unlikely rapid approach, every part of his body tense in anticipation. He was frightened to move in case he might scare her away. He spent much of his time being frightened, he realized then, while he followed her flickering steps that brought her closer to him. She wove amongst the trees, making his daily struggle through the growth look like a joyful game.

Even his chest rose and fell slowly, carefully. He didn't blink, not even when a bead of sweat broke through his eyebrow. The sweat stung his eyeball. He blinked, only once.

She was running as if all her days were different and there was reason to hurry through life to experience more and better, or just as good. She leapt as she stepped, and she gave him visions of her bouncing body through the screens of trees. The ends of her springing hair. A thigh. A full breast. A hand that whipped past incredibly fast.

When finally she reached him atop his tree stump, all words and thoughts eluded him, all but one. This must be love, he imagined, although he had never been in love before. His breath came shallow; he was sweating more than usual; and he felt as if he might faint. Either it was love, or he was having a heart attack.

She came to a stop right in front of him; there could be no doubt that she was there to see him. She had been running fast, yet her breath came normal and steady. He was certain of it because, with him seated, her chest lined up with his eyes.

He didn't want to move his eyes from her round breasts and their rhythmic, slow movement up and down, though he knew he would have to. He would have to find those rich brown eyes again. He had to. It was her eyes that he most remembered, half a year since he last saw her.

She waited for him as he had waited for her. She didn't shift with discomfort. She didn't know how to be uncomfortable. Things either were or they weren't; that was it.

She was fully naked. Nothing distracted from her beauty. She was born into this world naked, and had no reason to conceal her nakedness.

She appreciated her body, just as she appreciated the panther's sleek body, made for every one of its movements, and just as she loved the blooms of the orchids, pregnant with color, and the stiff form of the stick insect that blended in so precisely with the leaves and branches it lived among. Her body, like all the life within nature, was made to fulfill a purpose, and there were no mistakes in the designs of nature.

It didn't bother her when the man, forgetting himself entirely, trailed his eyes along every part of her body. He traced her curves, memorizing every one as much as he could, commanding himself to remember every piece of her.

Finally, the man found her eyes. His breathing calmed. His pulse grew steady.

He stayed within those eyes as long as she allowed him. And she did, for a long time, until the intensity of the moment became too much for the man.

Insanity, if she were not real, had become a distant consideration. He knew, nevertheless, that he could lose himself in the world that she encompassed. He didn't know how he knew it, but he did. Whoever she was, she gave off a raw power that he had never faced before, and that only the strong could survive.

He didn't touch her.

When he stared into the brown of her eyes for so long that he couldn't have told her his name if she'd asked, she took one step back, said nothing, and walked away.

From where he sat, he followed every sway of her hair, every bounce of her buttocks, and every flash of the soles of her feet, until she vanished. This time, he didn't think the jungle swallowed her.

The jungle embraced her as if welcoming one of its own.

CHAPTER FOUR

A Good Way to Die

WHEN his fellow workers came back and found him sitting on the stump, he didn't care to make it look as if he had been working the entire time they were gone. He would have told them that the woman appeared again had they asked, but they didn't. They just picked up their saws and got back to work, in their usual silent camaraderie.

He would have told the other villagers too. But no one asked. The woman's initial appearance had receded into legend, and few discussed her anymore. It had become one of those things that faded into the background of food harvesting and preparation, of living and dying.

Not even his parents, aunt, uncles, or grandmother asked him whether he had seen the woman of the jungle again. They had routines according to gender and age, and nothing varied them much.

With this secret he hadn't meant to keep secret, he began to feel like an outsider. And the more no one asked him about the woman, the more intent he became on keeping her to himself.

Although he didn't mention her again, she was never absent from his thoughts. Her brown eyes hovered behind the reality his eyes took in, always there, calling her to him.

He took to drifting away from the others. Now that he confirmed she was out there, that someone like her existed, certain things changed. His fear was less acute, his worries further removed from his mind. He longed for her, wishing that everything other than her would disappear. Nothing else was necessary.

She was like a narcotic. He walked around sedate. The chain saw felt detached from his calloused hands, as if it moved all by itself. Everything around him seemed to go on without his interaction with it. Time ticked on. Plants died and were reborn through their seedlings. Animals killed and gave birth.

She answered his call much sooner next time, the third time, which allowed him to hope that there might be even more to come.

She appeared as if in response to his wish. As always, as if it were the only way she could reach him, she approached through the dense jungle. He saw bits of her until she eventually coalesced into one whole in front of him, reawakening the desperate yearning for her within him.

She smiled at him, and instantly he realized that she had never smiled at him before. This was a smile meant for him, perhaps even caused by him, though he didn't know what he could have done to earn it. He smiled back. Two of his teeth on the bottom were crooked, but he forgot about that because he knew she wouldn't notice. Or if she noticed, she wouldn't care. Already, he could tell things like that about her.

He stood now, chain saw halfway through the trunk of an ancient tree; it was thick, and he was tired from trying to cut through it. He knew that moment so well, when the laboring teeth of the saw tore through the last of what needed to be cut, and broke free. Suddenly without challenge, the chain saw felt too light.

Without moving his eyes from her, he reached to power off the saw. Even though the blade vibrated with alarming danger, he felt for the off lever by memory and touch. He was already a changed man, after only three encounters.

He left the saw in the trunk, sticking out from it, hanging, like an error in the always-perfect design of nature. It was an aberration, though he didn't notice it then as he would later.

Despite the chain saw and the sweat and grime that covered him, she beamed a smile that was enough to wipe it all away.

He dared to breathe, more comfortable in her presence, less anxious that she might disappear as quickly and unpredictably as she had arrived. He took one small step toward her; it was barely anything at all, yet he held his breath to see what she would do, so close to him.

She didn't step back. She reached a hand out to him instead.

"I missed you," she said in her rhythmic Portuguese.

He couldn't believe his good fortune. Nothing truly fortunate had happened to him in his life. It had all been so ordinary. Yet there was nothing ordinary about his life now. It was impossible to look into those brown eyes and have a single ordinary thought.

"I missed you too. I wondered if you would come back."

She smiled again, but this time the smile held something he couldn't yet understand. "Of course I returned. I have been waiting for you for a long time. I have been searching for you. I always recognize you."

He took her hand and barely heard the meaning of her words for the distraction of her touch. Her skin was warmer than his and, somehow, felt more alive. Yet she did not sweat. A constant rivulet of sweat ran down the curve of his back, sometimes pooling in the small of it, sometimes not, beginning in the morning and only stopping at nighttime, and sometimes not even then. She, however, looked crisp and composed, as if she were walking in a different world, even though she looked like she belonged in the jungle more than he did.

She began to move, leading him by the hand. She could have led him anywhere, and he would have followed. Her touch was just enough to let him know that she was real and not a fiction of his deluded imagination.

He walked behind her. His eyes traveled over each ridge of her body, confirming that he remembered it correctly, that nothing had changed the perfection he'd relived many times since their last encounter. He didn't even hesitate when he realized where she was taking him. There came a point in life when one just had to let go of everything, and it seemed that this was that time.

She didn't slow, and it looked as if she were heading straight into the Amazon River with him tagging along behind her. But then, with her toes already wet, she turned. He ran into her—not much, but enough for the curves of her breasts to caress the cotton of his shirt, for the arc of her hip to brush against the leather of his belt. With difficulty, he dragged his eyes upward to meet hers.

She was about to speak, but in the end, did not.

He was about to speak, but thought better of it. If he should die now in that water, then it would be a good way to die. With her, any way of living or dying was better than what he could accomplish alone.

With her still facing him, he let go of her hand. Immediately, he missed it, as if a part of himself were gone. But it would only be for a moment.

He removed his work boots. They were too thick and stifling for the tropical weather, but the added protection was worth it. He left his socks in his boots with more elegance than their grime might have deserved. He unbuckled his belt, looped it carefully, and tucked it into his shoe.

He met her eyes again, this woman he didn't know. What a woman she was.

He pulled his shirt over his head and folded it atop his boots. Then, his long pants. Despite her nakedness, he stopped there. He stood in tattered underwear and retook her hand.

Then she pulled on his hand and walked into the water. She led the man who had been fearful of the Amazon all his life into the deep waters of that most dreaded river.

And he never came back. All that was left of him for the townspeople of Guayucuma were his boots, piled with his old, hard-worn clothing—that, and a legend that joined him inextricably with the woman.

CHAPTER FIVE

Death of a Way of Life

BEFORE long, the villagers declared the man dead, another victim of the jungle's greed and insatiability. The clearing around Guayucuma grew larger with each cycle of the moon. The light of each full, silver moon shone on less entangled tree canopies. The reaching sprawl that alighted magically from treetop to treetop had died somewhere, slain by the sputter of a saw.

A few people mourned the man. His parents, aunt, uncles, and grandmother shed tears for a handful of days. Then, they moved on. They were seasoned to accept losses. It was how life had always been for them—hard—and they saw no way around it. It was the way of their people. It always had been, even when their people still lived in the big city.

The man's aunt gave birth to a new generation, and she moved into his portion of the hut. She and her husband and the baby needed the extra space until they could build a hut of their own.

Life went on. A boy had matured into adulthood, and he took the man's boots and his place in the logging crew. He picked up the chain saw, still halfway through the ancient tree, and cut the tree all the way down.

With all the open space now, the villagers turned to gardening. They were surrounded by plenty, by lushness, but they sowed seeds of plants they trusted, of those which humans had domesticated generations before. They dug their fingers into the rich loam that released the scent of fertility every time they moved it, and they found their version of contentment in the Amazon rainforest.

Perhaps the man's death had placated the voracious spirit of the forest, and they would all be safe for some time. The man had been young and strong, virile and full of life. Surely that meant more to the jungle than the life of a crazy old woman, or any of the other strays that the jungle had taken. None had been such a hard worker. Even the man's parents thought it a worthy sacrifice, now that it had been done and there was nothing they could do to change it.

After a few weeks, no one spoke the man's name anymore. He had served his purpose, and the townspeople would continue to serve what they could understand of theirs, until death claimed them all.

CHAPTER SIX

The Silence of a Full Heart

"DO you not want to know my name?" the man asked the woman.

They had spent months in togetherness. They built a hut in a remote part of the jungle, where no one from Guayucuma dared go. Here, the rainforest was denser than in most other places. The animal life was more concentrated. The Amazon River diverted and plunged into a thrashing waterfall that those from Guayucuma didn't even know about.

"Names are not important. They can deceive. What you are made of cannot." She placed a warm palm against his bare chest.

He had abandoned thoughts of clothing soon after they arrived in this isolated area. No one but she would ever see him here.

"And what of your name? Do you have one?"

She drew a spiral across his chest with her finger, distractedly, he thought. "I have many names. But none that matters."

"Will you tell me your names if I want you to?"

"Yes. I will do most things if you want me to do them."

She sat and took her hand from his chest. She looked out from under their open-air casita into the jungle around them. They were nestled in the density of the forest, as if they were a part of it—She was, but was he?

He tilted his head back against the jute mat they had woven together, once she taught him how. She didn't do things like the women from his village did. She didn't do things like anyone else he knew, or had once known.

She culled jute that was dying and broke it into long strands. Once, he reached for a plant that was thriving, and she grabbed his wrist until he let go; then she softened her touch.

She hadn't let him cut down a single tree either. Their casita was squeezed into a small natural clearing of the forest, butting against trees and plants on all sides, like a tree house that couldn't take flight. Only once, he suggested he return for his chain saw to clear ample room for them, but the suggestion died with a look from those brown eyes.

He sat and scooted up against her, his chest pressing against her back. He put his forehead and cheek on that warm flesh, and he forgot all about names and the many she might have. Throughout all the time they shared, he would never ask again. There were days when he nearly forgot his own.

It was easy to forget things that were unimportant, even though they had been important to him once, not so long ago. All the fears that had consumed him before he met the woman went away so easily that he couldn't even find evidence of the deep roots he was sure they cast into him. He borrowed her courage.

He had made it across that beastly river, the Amazon, unscathed, and had survived every other day just as re-markably, accompanied by her. His life was divided into two distinct parts: life without her and life with her. He hoped there would never be a third.

Early on she had asked him if he missed his family and his village, if he wanted to return. He didn't, and so she had gone on to teach him how to make their casita a home. She showed him how to secure a good roof to it, and it was a roof better than any of the huts of Guayucuma had. Again, they gathered jute that was dead or dying, and together they wove. Once they secured the roof onto the frame, not one drop moistened the ground from above; it only crept up from below.

Their hut was secure and provided all the shelter they needed, although it was mostly bare. When he lived in Guayucuma, he had grown accustomed to making the most of the little he had. His needs weren't many. Now, living with this woman, he realized his needs were even fewer than he had believed them to be.

The more time he spent with her, the more her view of the world around them colored his own. She spoke little, and so he did too. Her words were sparse, but precise, and he learned to interpret everything she said and did to discover its deeper meaning.

She taught him to survive in the jungle, one of the most dangerous places on earth, as if it contained no real perils. He couldn't understand how the animals didn't threaten her. Stories of snake charmers and tiger tamers had traveled to Guayucuma from the big city. They were all different versions of the same worn tales, and he had never considered them really true, just stories meant to entertain the children and those bored of routine.

The woman could be a snake charmer and a tiger tamer, if only she wanted to be. On his first full day with her, he had seen enough to believe any outrageous story or legend he had ever heard. She walked through the forest as master of it. But no, it wasn't that, although the animals flocked to her as if she were their gentle master. It was something else. She was part of the forest. No matter where she was or what she was doing, she became a part of everything greater that surrounded her.

He tried to imitate her. He attempted to glide through the thick growth as if nothing were in his way. He actually expected the gnarled roots and branches to clear for him. Yet they didn't. The roots were surprise tripping hazards; it didn't matter that he knew they were everywhere around him. The branches hung too low, and he was constantly jumping back from one that reached for his eyes.

Several times he stood still, letting her move far beyond him, just watching her. He would have sworn that the roots and branches moved out of her way, the flock making its magic available to its leader. But it wasn't so. The roots and branches were as fixed as they were for him. Yet she never startled; she never tripped. All of her movements were graceful, as if she knew every bump, leaf, and trunk, as if she had created them herself.

She walked gingerly through the trees, running gentle fingertips across leaves and flowers as she passed, stopping to hold a particularly handsome tree trunk. After so much time spent with her, the man began to appreciate some of the beauty as well, but still his focus remained on the sway of her black hair as it swung across her waist and upper buttocks, reflecting the sun that filtered through the heavy canopy above in a shiny black-blue. Her beauty was as magnificent as anything around them, greater even than the dangling orchid with its brilliant pinks and oranges that could match any sunset.

The woman stopped to take in the orchid. She smiled, not at him but at the flower, and rubbed a thumb and forefinger across the silk of one petal.

Without a word, she resumed walking, knowing that he would follow. He always followed. There was no reason to pretend he could lead through the Amazon better than she did. He watched her footfalls. He stepped where she stepped, around poisonous snakes and insects, and avoiding animal homes and sprouting plants that were building their strength.

She took him to the waterfall, where the rushing water roared so loudly that it forced out any extraneous thought. She climbed and ducked under the waterfall, and took a seat, leaning against slippery, moss-covered stone. Water, unreasonably powerful water, streamed in front of them, cascading across the opening that would have otherwise been air. The water never slowed and it never wavered, plummeting with great force.

No human could jump into that waterfall and survive. It wasn't the lurking predators in the water that would kill you; the innate violence of water traveling in such quantity and at such speed would crush the life out of anyone so daring, or so stupid. If these last months with the woman had taught him anything, it was that life, even minute life, was precious.

If they had wanted to speak, they would have had to shout to be heard. They rarely spoke anyway. Life around them was so vivid that he didn't even mind the long silences anymore. He discovered that he heard more when he didn't speak, and especially when he didn't think of what he might say. When it became still and quiet inside, he found room for those things he had never imagined could fulfill him.

Today was no different. He sank into the wet stone behind him and welcomed the spray the falls misted across his sweaty skin. He leaned his head back and felt the power of the waterfall surging and vibrating through the rock beneath him. Without lifting his head, he passed her a papaya he had picked on the way.

He still knew so little about her. He didn't know her name and never would. He didn't know what tribe she was from or how she came to be apart from it, or how she had learned to speak Portuguese. He didn't know what happened to her family; she must have one, some- where, even if only bones beneath dirt. He didn't even know how old she was, though he guessed she was his age.

He had thought of seeking answers to these ques- tions before, and had considered many more than these. Yet every time he came to the point of asking, when he thought he finally would learn more about her, something within urged him not to, or they moved onto another subject, and the opportunity passed. Those facts that before had been so important as to be defining, didn't seem worth bothering about now.

He wouldn't feel any different about her once he knew them. He didn't need to know, really. Or was it that he was afraid that her answers might somehow spoil this idyllic peace that they shared in one of the world's most dangerous wildernesses? It seemed too good to be true in most ways, and he didn't want to prove it so.

He had given up all that he knew of life before her to sit behind a raging waterfall, naked, with ripe, hot papaya juice dripping down his hands, arms, and stomach.

He learned all that he needed about her by the way she walked and smiled. The way she caressed flower petals and petted monkeys revealed more than a million words. It was within the silence of a full heart that he found love—true, passionate, tender, hungry love—for the first time. It was here that he discovered who he was and who he might dream of becoming.

CHAPTER SEVEN

Part of the Whole

IT was difficult to keep track of the lapsing of time. At first, the man counted the days. That was easy enough; the sun would rise on a new day, one of the few reliable constants in an ever-changing life. But once the figure reached into the hundreds, he couldn't recall what number he was on, and he grew suspicious that he had forgotten to count other days as well.

By the time he reached the five hundreds, he knew his count to be highly inaccurate and was surprised to discover that he didn't particularly care to know how much time had passed. The certainty was that it had passed, and that time didn't mind whether he counted it or not.

What he could more readily keep track of was how he was changing. After several years—somewhere between three and five—he no longer needed to follow the woman everywhere to feel safe. Some of her ways had turned out to be contagious and, gradually, he had be-come more tranquil inside. Inner stillness turned out to be the great secret to connecting with the forest the way she did—or at least, he thought that was the secret to how she walked the jungle as a harmonious part of it.

Tranquility was inevitable amid her silence, and his, and the constant thrumming life of the jungle. He would have had to work to keep his mind trapped in its waste-ful loop of endless thoughts that meant nothing in the end. And he had no reason to want that. His mind felt freer than it ever had, and the rainforest seemed like the ideal home for a free mind.

The woman taught him well. She monitored his ac-tions closely until she was certain that he could uphold the principles of balance and respect that meant more to her than names and facts. The details she cared about didn't need names, or even words; they could be con-tained fully in the rich color of a butterfly wing or the flesh of a frog, with its array of saturated pigment.

This was to be one of the rare occasions when she spoke to him at length, even saying things a few differ-ent ways to make sure he understood. They were out walking, harvesting food items as they passed. They didn't need much, and there was no need to store food for later. Food was abundant, ripe and juicy, waiting to be plucked from a nearby branch.

The woman drew around to one of the trees she returned to frequently in their walks. It was one of the oldest. Its trunk was thick, seeping wisdom from every bump in its bark and from every gnarled, exposed root. She loved it. She had never said so, but she didn't need to. She lit up when she was next to this tree.

"Will you join me?" she said as she began scaling the tree. It had wide, low-hanging branches that curved as if they had been designed for lounging.

He didn't answer with words anymore, not usually. He climbed and took a seat across from her. She straddled the branch and leaned back. She was made for this kind of thing—but then, it was as if the tree had been made for her. She always found the most comfortable perches, the most perfect fruit, and the slowly running water of peaceful inlets.

He straddled the same limb and also leaned back. The tree branch was comfortable, yet it didn't curve as if molded to his back. Not like it did for her.

He was used to it, to the differences between them. He couldn't imagine he would ever become like her. And he was okay with that. He preferred it actually, to leave that special something that only she possessed as hers alone. He folded his arms across his chest contentedly and tilted his face toward the flickering sunlight above.

"She is a beautiful mother tree, isn't she?"

It wasn't a real question, and he wasn't certain if she was talking to him or to the tree. He didn't ask. He didn't always understand what she did, or what little she said, but he was accustomed to that. When he didn't comprehend the deeper meaning of her actions or words right away, he often would sometime later, even if it was a long time later. Her ways always possessed significance; if he couldn't see it, then he just hadn't seen it yet.

"You have learned to do things the way I do them, and that is good. It is good that you respect the jungle.

"I want you to know why I honor the forest as I do, so you can choose to do it for yourself, not just because of my example."

A lizard met eyes with her, as if asking for permission, then climbed onto her hand. She lifted him close to her face and held him there, admiring him while she ran a finger along the length of his back, down to the narrow tip of his tail.

"The forest is alive. It is not just the life that you can observe breathing and moving; it is everything. It is the moss and the grasses; the fruit fly, the spider, the worm, and the ant; as much as it is the jaguar and the puma. As much as it is this tree.

"Life runs through everything in this jungle as it does through everything else on earth. As it does within you." She shifted her eyes from the lizard to the man, across from her. He watched her, mesmerized by her interaction with their surroundings and by the lilting music of her voice.

"That is why I do not take the life of anything for granted. It is why I step carefully and why I do not take anything that is not ready for me to take. There is a moment when every living thing can be plucked from its mother, when it has served its purpose, or it is ready to serve its purpose by offering itself to another life form.

"But it is not for man to take without honor or to interrupt the natural cycle of life."

Her eyes returned to the lizard. "Man is no greater than this lizard, or this tree, or a leech. Every one of you serves a purpose that is necessary for balance. Every purpose is important. Every part is."

She was finished speaking. Already, it was more than she had ever said to him at one time. Still, he didn't have anything to offer in reply, and he was grateful that she didn't expect him to surmount the thick lump of emotion in his throat. It wasn't the few sentences she had voiced; it was rather all that she had not.

And it was also something that he couldn't readily identify. It was something that was bubbling up inside him, but that he didn't understand, and was too upset to try. He didn't know why, but the emotions gurgling up in response to her words were part shame and part admiration, and the two weren't usually a match.

She released the lizard on the limb behind her and scooted forward toward him. "It is when man trusts nature that nature begins to trust man." She kissed him on the cheek; one of his tears wet her lips. It was the gentle, compassionate kiss of a mother.

Then she scuttled around him and down the tree with the dexterity of monkeys, and continued ambling through the forest without him.

For once, he didn't look down to follow her path or to enjoy the beauty of her body. He closed his eyes against a wave of feeling that was threatening to crash inside him, even if he didn't yet know the reasons why.

CHAPTER EIGHT

The Seed

THE woman didn't talk to the man about the importance of honoring the rainforest again, nor did she ask him his thoughts about what she had said. But she did monitor what he did less closely. She didn't hover over him when he was picking fruit or reeds or sticks. Her hand didn't wait next to his to interfere before he cut down something alive.

She sensed him walking more carefully behind her. Now, his steps didn't just evade what might hurt him. New shoots survived, small, delicate threads that were only just beginning to weave an intricate tapestry that would soar to the heights of the forest. Towering trees began with just one seed. All of life did, and for the first time in his entire life, the man thought about the seed from which he had grown.

There was so much that was crystallizing within him that he didn't know if he could grasp it. Perhaps he would allow what was reshaping him to roll on through without understanding what was happening.

He became vulnerable and raw, and he thought he might understand what the caterpillar felt like transforming in its cocoon. He was shedding an old skin like a snake does.

When so much fell away from the man he had been—before she found him that first time in the jungle, next to his chain saw—what was left beneath was fragile, desiring protection and consideration. He didn't know who he would become after the process was complete, when he emerged from the cocoon a butterfly.

So he tried not to think about it, and that was not difficult in the rainforest. It was especially easy with her. Like the animals around them, he trusted her; there had never been a question whether he could. She was the right one to feel vulnerable with, to witness the new, soft baby flesh.

He could give himself to her without fear when they made love. He gave to her freely, because he knew she never took too much. The jungle knew it too.

It was on one of these hot, sticky days when they gave themselves to their love that she anticipated his question. She always did. She watched the desire cross his eyes and recognized it for what it was each time.

She wasn't surprised. She never was. It was innate in him as it was in all life across the earth, the planet she knew as intimately as she knew him.

She could have spoken his question before he did, words and all. "Why can we not create a child together?" It was a sensible request, with him deep inside her, the way humans were designed to continue the cycle of life, yet it was worded in a way that preceded her answer. Even though everything about her echoed the fertility that was apparent everywhere in nature—her hips were round, her breasts full, her abdomen anticipating the swell of life that could grow within her—he knew what her answer would be.

It made no sense, he thought even before she spoke. "This body is not meant to bear your child."

"But of course it is." He ran his hands convincingly across her breasts, her back, her buttocks, and finally rested on her hips, encouraging her to continue her rocking forward and backward. She enjoyed it as much as he did. It was how they spent much of their days.

Having babies was what people did. At least, it had been in Guayucuma. When boys and girls became young men and women, it was time for them to marry. After a short time, they would begin their own families. It was how it was done. It is undoubtedly what he would have done had he stayed in the village.

As soon as he saw her, he realized that he wanted to live out his life with her. It didn't matter that they were nearly strangers. There were some things people just knew, and the length of time knowing someone had nothing to do with them.

Once they became lovers, he thought family would become a natural progression of their union. But the days passed—this was when he still counted them—and her abdomen retained its roundness but did not swell further.

"I have borne too many children already. I will not give birth to more in this body. I cannot."

"Why can you not? We love each other, do we not? Shouldn't that be all that is needed to create a child? We will love the child as we love each other. We will raise the baby in the jungle. It will be beautiful."

"It would be beautiful. I know that. But I still cannot."

"I do not understand."

"I know you don't, and I am sorry. But I am already mother to too many. I cannot shirk my responsibilities to the children I already have to change who and how I am to have a child with you." It was a similar answer to the one she had given him many times before.

He was about to ask why some more. Why, why, why? The words had already formed on his lips. But then she did something different with her hips and he couldn't think anymore, and a moan slid from his lips, not at all the words he'd intended.

"This is how it has always been for us. It is how it must be, because of who you are and because of who I am."

"And who are you and who am I?"

"You are man and I am mother."

He was nearing the point when thought of any kind was nearly impossible, and if it was possible, he didn't want it to replace the sensation of overpowering bliss that was building inside him, stretching toward her, wanting to share its beauty with her.

"Do you still choose me? If we cannot have a child together, not now or ever, do you still want a life with me over one with a woman who can give you the family that you want?"

He pulled away from the brilliant light that would burst behind his eyelids at any moment, the one that he was anticipating, savoring even before it arrived. His eyelids gave a swift flutter open, but that was sufficient for him to see what she wanted for him: happiness whether with her or without her. If he wanted a family, she didn't want to deny him that. He was free to have children with someone else.

He closed his eyes again before she saw the one last flickering thought, before there was nothing more than that light. There could be no someone else. There could only be her. For him, that's how it would always be.

"There can only be you for me."

She nodded, her black hair swinging wildly, as free as she was. He didn't see it. He was feeling her, and there was so much of her to feel, too much to contain.

She leaned into him and moved her hips side to side. Heavy breasts pressed against his chest. She whispered with palpable breath next to his ear. "Then it is as it has always been for us. It has always been just you and me. No one else."

He couldn't hold back any longer. He didn't know if he would have wanted to had he been able. He released every bit of himself within her, sharing everything he had to offer with her.

Everything he had, everything of his that she wanted, was hers.

She gripped his thighs with her own, then collapsed against his chest. Their breathing heavy and hot, their hair intermixing, almost the same color, his beginning to grow long like the vines of the forest.

He trailed a fingertip down the curve of her back, from the nape of her neck to the dip of her waist. Yes, life with her would be enough for him. He would not regret a moment shared with her.

He kissed her on the lips. It was a gentle kiss that spoke of promises already made long ago, long before he ever met her.

CHAPTER NINE

Trust Breeds Contentment

THAT time was the last that he brought up children, and before long, he didn't think about his life in terms of what he didn't have, but in terms of all that he did have. His blessings were more than he could want to count.

Only once did he ask, "Should we not at least get married?" As had become his way, he formed his question in the negative when a part of him already suspected what her answer would be. Still, he had to ask.

She laughed at this question, tilting her head back with amusement. Had he not known her better, he might have taken offense. The previous version of him, the one that cut down trees by the dozens every day, would have.

"Are we not married already? Marriage is no more than a promise between two people to love and share each other. Have we not made that promise to each other already, when we first met and every day since?"

They hadn't spoken the words, but she was right nonetheless; of course they had made promises to each other that were as binding within his heart as any contract of matrimony. "But under whose authority are we married?"

"Do we need an authority greater than our own? Do we need anything other than our hearts to speak for us?"

"I suppose not." But in Guayucuma they did. In the big city they did.

Her voice softened. "If we need something greater than ourselves to witness our promises and our love, is the jungle not sufficient? Is all the life within this forest not enough to bear witness? Is there any authority greater than the breath that cycles around the earth?"

His voice was even quieter. "No." She was right. She was already his wife. "And can we continue to make love even if we do not intend to create children?" He still hoped it might someday happen by accident, despite her intentions otherwise. If it were an accident, then she would know it was perfect. She always said there were no true accidents.

"Making love—creating love—needs no greater reason. Love is beautiful. It is the reason for living. Love is meant to be shared."

And so it was that the man and the woman—whose names neither one knew—shared many years together as husband and wife, as man and woman, as lovers of the heart. They lived in their protected portion of the forest, never traveling too far from it, never seeing another human being again.

They walked the forest. The man learned to navigate its thickness almost as easily as she. They harvested fruits and vegetables ready and willing to serve this purpose. They tended to the trees and the smaller plants and their flowers, to the animals, small and large, to the insects, to the miniscule, to everything there was.

The woman was the consummate gardener. The way she tended, and taught him to tend, was through appreciation. She said that appreciation was all that a plant needed to grow or an animal to thrive. All he and she needed to do was care and discover beauty.

Life in the rainforest became easeful. How could it not? Fear was gone, trust was everywhere, and beauty for him to appreciate was omnipresent. He slept in peace beneath the jute covering of their open-air casita, albeit now he understood that even this protection from the elements was unnecessary.

He didn't need to shield himself from the elements any longer. Nothing in nature was a threat to him, because he was no longer a threat to nature.

As he slept, his chest rose and fell in the placid type of sleep that comes from contentment. He didn't even notice that the woman left his side every night.

She slipped out into the inky jungle, with the different set of animals that came out of hiding under the cloak of darkness. She went home only once they did.

When the sun was about to rise, she would nestle back into her bed next to the man she always chose to love.

CHAPTER TEN

A Simple Winding Truth

TEDIUM was a constant risk for a resident of Guayucuma, a place so small it was dubious whether it should be called a town or have a name of its own. When the man lived there, each day had been similar to the previous one so as to seem almost identical: He woke, cut down trees all day, went home to the hut he shared with his extended family, and slept.

In the jungle, he couldn't say how each day differed from the last, and a succinct explanation of their routine might have given the impression that there was room for boredom, just as before. Yet there was not. It hadn't occurred to him that he might become bored, no matter how many days they spent in each other's company without speaking at all.

He had learned to see those small, less easily noticeable details of the jungle, much like she did. And it was these almost-secret details—hidden in plain sight—that gifted life with a richness that left no room for even the possibility of ennui.

Every day was filled with excursions. Whether they swam in the river—one of his favorite activities now that he no longer feared that a caiman or a piranha would sneak up under him—circled the waterfall, climbed a tree, or walked all day, they were surrounded by perfect balance and striking beauty.

The color combinations of the flowers, birds, and insects were so striking he was grateful he didn't need words to describe them. The constant animal calls and creaking of the forest had become comforting, proof of the vastness of life that surrounded them. The constant non-stop movement that was always somewhere near them reminded him that he was an important part of everything else, big and small.

The splendor that each sunrise and sunset revealed was the only thing to mark the days that passed. There was no more sense of time to the man, only a sense of beauty. The woman had gifted him more than a life shared with her; she had offered him true life. She had blessed his eyes with the ability to see, to really see! He could hear, taste, touch, and feel a richness he hadn't known existed.

Indeed, life had become so rich that he was surprised to discover that he had aged. The woman had not. She looked the same as she had when he first glimpsed her running behind the flickers of trees, except that she looked more beautiful to him.

The profoundness of her love, not just for him, but for everything—even the predator that eviscerated its gentle prey, just part of the balance of nature, she would say—made her the most radiant woman alive, and he was certain it must be true. There couldn't be anyone else like her. It wasn't possible.

One day, while he walked behind the firm buttocks and legs she had always had, long black, shiny hair still sweeping across them with each of her steps, he said, "I have aged. You have not."

She didn't say anything for a long time. He thought she wouldn't answer. She often didn't if she didn't think there was a need.

When her voice finally came, it was sad. He couldn't remember if he had ever heard sadness in her voice before. "Yes." A simple answer, laden with a truth that wasn't simple at all.

He thought about her "yes" for a while. He believed he had gotten quite good at reading in between the few lines they shared each day. He knew there was a lot to that one word; it was obvious.

Still, he eventually decided he didn't know what it was. Not precisely. "Why do I age when you do not?"

Again, the melancholy. "Because of who you are and because of who I am. I've told you before. You are man. I am mother."

That one other word, "mother," sent a surprise pang wobbling through him. It had been a long while since he had thought about the fact that he didn't have children. Now, he realized he had grown old—perhaps not old yet, but older—and it looked like he never would be a father.

"And why are you sad now?" When they discussed topics like these, if anyone was sad, it was him.

She didn't turn. She just kept walking, those youthful legs swinging hypnotically, leading him ever forward. When she finally answered, it was on a gasp that tried to subdue a sob. He wouldn't hear something like this from her again until they had reached the end.

"Because one day soon, you will die."

The end was coming sooner than he imagined, yet that wouldn't be the biggest of the surprises the end held for him.

CHAPTER ELEVEN

The Oblivion of Dreams

EVEN once the man realized that his mortality trailed him across the Amazon jungle like one of its great predators, he was able to forget about it most of the time. Death stalked him, a fleeting set of glowing eyes that disappeared too quickly when he turned to catch them, to verify that the feeling of being followed was real.

Still, he wasn't certain how much he really minded if he were to stop and think about it, which he did not. Long gone were the days when fears plagued him and stole thoughts from him. He lived amongst wild animals, where life and death were ever-present.

He was one of those wild animals now, and death would come to him as it did to them: when it was supposed to arrive. There was no point in resisting it.

His impermanence hung over him, but it did not weigh heavily. Instead, it served as a reminder of all there was to appreciate while still alive. And it was easier for him to bear the thought of his death when he knew that he would die before her.

She would pass from this world too, eventually, but he would not have to endure a life without her, a loss infinitely greater than death. He knew his heart could not stand to be apart from her. It would shatter, and he would be dead while still living; there was little worse than that.

So many years had passed them by, together in the jungle, that he barely remembered his life without her. Though he knew it made no sense, it didn't seem to him as if there had ever been life before her. It was as if it had always been just the two of them and an infinite world contained by the ancient trees that marked the periphery of this jungle.

He never left their remote area of the forest. He never again heard a human voice other than hers. They were too far away to overhear the back and forth shouts of the loggers, many more than there had been when he was one of them. The loggers, the most dangerous of all the stalkers, circled the rainforest each day, closing in on their removed setting and its thundering waterfall.

The threat was real. One day, loggers would deliver death upon the forest. They would show no mercy nor would they hesitate.

Beginning early, the loggers' chain saws buzzed their cacophony, drowning out the insects' morning songs. The insects sang anyway, because it was what they were made to do. The loggers could take away their home, but they couldn't take away their purpose.

The saws didn't stop until dusk. When they finally did, and the silence in their aftermath made the calls of the jungle unbearably real, the loggers left right away, to begin the long trek to their homes. The walk home took longer than it had before, when trees still circled their town. Now, the trees were farther removed, deeper in the heart of the forest that remained.

For fear of the forest and everything in it, loggers traveled in packs, like the man once had. Especially now that the animals' habitat had shrunk sharply, they were frightened. To them, the animals seemed out of balance and disoriented, more prone to attack men than ever before.

Every evening, when dusk obscured the sun, and the loggers finally arrived at their villages, they exhaled a deep sigh of relief. They hadn't been mauled. They were home where it was safe, where things made sense, and where there was an order they could understand: wake, eat, cut down trees, eat, cut down more trees, load logs onto trucks, walk home, eat, sleep.

They didn't realize that an order so much greater surrounded them. It functioned without them—much as it always had and much as it always would.

The man, deep in the jungle, where the sound of chain saws was still blissfully absent, where a bird's squawk could ring out across the stillness that was, paradoxically, brimming with life, was unaware that less of the jungle remained now than ever before. He didn't consider himself a logger anymore, and didn't think much about the cutting of trees.

He didn't perceive the death of the forest like he did his own. He knew his death would come, but it seemed impossible to consider that the forest could die. It teemed with life. There was too much of it. How could all that life ever die? Even if the answer—one tree at a time—had crossed his mind, it would have still seemed unachievable that so much richness could be extinguished.

The man didn't know. Vivid color, sound, and smell continued to surround him so that all that vibrancy extended to beat inside him too.

But the woman knew. She knew everything that he did not.

At night while he slept, she walked the jungle, *her* jungle. And every night, she mourned the losses. She knew that the man she loved would perhaps never fully understand. Or perhaps he would, but it would be too late. It already was. It had been for a long time, long even for her.

In yawning darkness or under the filtered light of the moon, the night animals of the forest surrounded her. They couldn't understand how deep the loss that she grieved was; they weren't made to. They were impervious to fear, independent from immediate threat. It was one of her favorite blessings of the animal and plant kingdoms. She was glad for them, as glad as she was of their company, knowing that they were perfect manifestations of perfect design.

Predators and prey congregated around her. It was how it had always been. Near her, animals could only act peacefully. It wasn't that she didn't give them a choice; she did, yet they always made the right one.

She let sadness and disappointment flow through her. She always imagined things could be different this time around. The same seed was planted in humans as in the rest of the animals. But the seed seemed to flourish consistently only in the animals.

For most humans, the seed died shortly after germination. And in those that the seed shot strongly upward, reaching toward the light, where it eventually flowered, there were too few able to appreciate the powerful beauty of its bloom.

Yet, there was absolutely nothing wrong with the seed. She was absolutely certain of this. And that was why her walk back to the lean-to she shared with the man she chose to love was always slower than on her way out. On the walk back, there was more concern to leave behind.

He never noticed the difference in her from the night to the morning. He hadn't realized that she left every single night.

There was so much that he didn't realize. It had ceased to surprise her a long time ago.

This morning, when she lined herself up next to him on their shared jute mat, she didn't close her eyes. Closed eyelids would do nothing to push away the images of the dying jungle she took in every night while he slept.

She waited for the sun to rise. It would happen soon.

In the light of the new sun, she followed the lines across his face and neck. She especially loved when two lines intersected, when they tangled to become more expressive than just one of them could by itself.

His skin was creased with the stories of age. She knew every one of them by heart; she had been with him as he gave birth to each new adventure. The later ones were deeper, carved across his handsome face.

She never woke him when he slept. She knew better than anyone that the rhythms of sleep, aligned with the rising and setting of the sun, were an essential part of human balance. But today, after so many years, she reached out one soft, warm finger to trace a wrinkle from the corner of his eye to where it met his cheek. She followed the groove that trailed down the side of his mouth. These were the evidence of the many smiles they had shared.

She could remember every single one of them. They were part of what made her nighttime tears bearable.

He shifted and she lifted her finger, hovering her hand above him, waiting for his alertness to pass. It did, and he turned away from her, still mostly asleep. She moved against him. She pressed her breasts, abdomen, and thighs against his back and buttocks. His skin was warm and inviting from deep sleep.

Once his breathing regained its rhythm, she closed her eyes. He would fully wake soon. He slept only a short time past sunrise. For whatever time she had, she allowed herself to fall asleep too. She joined him in the oblivion of forgetfulness and dreams.

It was the first time she had slept in years. That morning, she wanted any sort of dream to come along. It would be preferable to the reality that swept across the planet like a fever, contagious and threatening the onset of terrible and irreversible changes. In her dream, only a mirage of relief, she dreamt that the planet broke out in fever blisters.

CHAPTER TWELVE

The Sound of a Breaking Heart

ORE time passed. It always did. There was nothing the man could do to stop it.

He was old now. His age announced itself as soon as he woke each morning, when one of the first things he felt was the ache and creak of his bones and joints while he stretched the sleep from his body.

But it was not the very first thing. Before he even opened his eyes, he felt the expanding love in his heart for the woman he considered his wife and for the jungle that provided everything they needed.

She had changed him a long time ago, and he remained a changed man. He could see through pain and tragedy to what lay beneath. Ultimately, behind it all, even when it didn't appear possible, there was beauty.

When he looked at her, illuminated by the soft light of dawn, he knew the day had come. He was surprised, even though he had known it was coming. He couldn't argue with the signs his body had been giving him for some time, nor did he try.

He no longer accompanied her on walks that took up most of their day. It was too much for him. He would join her halfway, then sit until her return, enjoying his own slice of time in the forest.

She had been waiting for him to wake as she often did. Lately, it seemed that he woke most days to find her gazing at him with love in her brown eyes. He looked back at her, wondering exactly how many more moments like this were left to him.

He thought he understood. She knew this day would come. She might have even known it would be this day.

Today he would die.

Her brown eyes, the ones he could never get enough of, foreshadowed that exacting reality. He hadn't thought he would mind knowing death was coming, but now that it was upon him, he wished he could hide where death would not find him. The thought of never staring into those eyes again was making his breath come short and raspy.

Was it the thought of losing that brown stare, or was it death, coming to get him so early, robbing him of his last full day? It didn't seem fair that death could cheat him of a final day. Death should never be allowed to take you before you lived out your last day on earth to its fullest.

The man squelched unexpected desperation, tamping it down, back to the shadowy corner from which it had escaped. If it could only stay there for a few more hours, he would never have to deal with it.

Everything looked different than he thought it would now that death was closing in on him.

The woman, the one that had changed him in a way that perhaps not even death could erase, leaned over him. Her breasts dangled heavily above his face until she positioned herself to help him sit.

He leaned against one of the tree trunks that demarcated the perimeter of their home. He smiled at her. It was a weak smile, but it didn't matter. It carried just as much love for her as his smiles always did.

"I am going to die today, aren't I?"

"No," she said, though the sad shake of her head defied the truth of her words.

He waited. He could feel death coming.

"But today I will leave you."

A seed of frantic panic sprung out of nowhere in his stomach. How could that seed be there without his knowing?

"What do you mean you will leave me?" He drew the question out slowly, delaying as much as he could the answer that would inevitably come.

"I do not want to go. But I must." She forced herself to look at him while she spoke. She knew what it would be like for him when she left. She knew exactly how much courage it would take for him to face death without her. She would not shy away from her choices; she couldn't do that to him.

Something plummeted within him, something that he couldn't quite describe. If he were forced to, he would have to say that a part of him died right at that moment. And if it didn't, it wanted to.

"Do you really mean it?" He slumped against the tree behind him; it was the only thing holding him up. "Will you really leave me?" His words were little more than a whisper. Anything louder than that might have made them more true.

"Yes." And in the profound sadness and resignation he found in her eyes, he knew that she would.

He didn't expect it of himself, but he didn't know how to stop it. Cries slipped, broken like he was, from his lips. It was as if it weren't him making those awful sounds, almost inhuman. It was the sound of his breaking heart.

She was so much stronger than he was. He didn't know if she had aged at all since he first met her. He had been certain that she would outlive him a hundred times over, and that she would be there with him at the end, to lend him her strength when he began the journey that every human had to make alone.

The thought that she wouldn't be there with him for his transition was equally startling and unbearable. How could she do this to him? After all they had shared together, why would she make this choice?

He couldn't face her while he lay, weak and shattered, against a tree that would also outlive him. He couldn't look into those brown eyes while his heart completed its breaking.

The sounds that poured out of him regained their humanity, and then settled into heaviness and sniffles. Still, he didn't want to look at her. The betrayal was too great to meet those eyes he had lost himself in so many times before and not risk all the memories of their time together. Regardless of what he felt now, he cherished those memories. It was all he had left. He would not risk coloring them with a betrayal he could not understand.

She waited, sitting next to him, just holding his hand, nothing more. That was enough, to know she was there with him, that she cared. It was all he had expected of her at the time of his death. What she was doing now would have been sufficient for him.

When the tears dried, and he still wouldn't look at her, she reached up one warm hand, its flesh still smooth, and turned his head to face her. It was a tender movement, gentle as she had always been with him—until now. There was nothing gentle about breaking his heart.

"I do not want to leave you. I never do. This is as difficult for me as it is for you."

In all the time they had shared together, he had never seen her cry. He hadn't cried either. There had been no reason to until now.

When he looked into her face, he discovered the trails of tears dried against her cheeks, lines of white against that beautiful brown. She stared at him intently. "I will leave you only because I must."

The man worked hard to contain another wave of sorrow, more mighty than a tsunami that threatened to swell within him. He didn't know anymore if he was there or not, or whether sometime since his lover had started speaking that morning, his broken heart had actually killed him.

He didn't care about living out the rest of this day anymore. All he could think about was how it would feel to be without her.

When he spoke, he was numb. "What could make you leave me? Is there something more important than the love that we have shared for so many years?"

She smiled a sorrowful smile. Everything she did now seemed to transmit her regret when he had never seen her truly sad before this day. "There are many things more important to this world than our love, many responsibilities that must take precedence."

Even more hurt flashed across his face before finding a place to hide within him. Finally, she lowered her hand from his cheek, but only to place it on his chest above his heart. "But there is little more beautiful or important to me than our love."

"What is more important to you than our love that you must leave me at the time of my greatest need?"

"It is not what is more important to you or me. That is not the correct question for the answer you seek. It is because my love for you is so great that I must leave you. I cannot watch you die."

The hurt within him unclenched for just a moment, hopeful.

"Why can't you watch me die? Is it because it would be hard for you?" He placed a hand atop hers, and even through it, he could feel the desperate beating of his heart.

"It is because it would be so difficult for me that I might do something terrible."

He squeezed her hand. "You wouldn't take your life. I know you too well. You may fear it now, but you value life too much to do it. The thought of it would pass."

"I would never end my own life. My life is tied to countless others. There is a greater reason. I cannot watch you die because I might try to save you."

"That is understandable. I would feel the same if our roles were reversed. I would want desperately to save you."

"I know I will want to save you, because I always do. It has been the same with us every time. I want to save you. And I never can."

"My love, you do not have to leave me because you cannot save me. It is how life is. When death comes for us, we must go. There is nothing you can do to change that."

"I am not like you. I have told you many times. You and I are different. I *can* save you. And I cannot allow myself to do that."

She slid her hand out from under his and stood. She left him there, against the tree trunk.

As he watched her leave him behind, he hoped she would be back. He hoped this wasn't the end. He couldn't bear it if it were. He wasn't sure he could bear it even if it wasn't.

CHAPTER THIRTEEN

Hiding in Plain Sight

HE waited all day long for her to return so he could ask her one question. In all the time she left him to think, he came up with theories—not all of them plausible and none of them accurate—and different ways to phrase his pressing need to know.

When she finally came back, he blurted it out. If she had meant to greet him, he didn't give her the chance. "What do you mean, you can save me?"

She sighed. It always came down to this with them. She sat across from him and crossed her legs. He had barely moved all day, and he was back to resting against the tree where she had left him. Death was coming for him, and his body knew it. He stored his energy for when he would need it, even if it was only for crossing the line between life and death.

She sat with a straight back, with the strength and vitality of youth. She exhaled before she began. "I can save your life."

Why didn't she want to save him then? Again, hurt rushed up his spine, aiming for his brain and for his heart as if it were a race it intended to win. This time, however, the man pushed it down and waited.

"I can save your life, but at great cost. And it is a cost too great to bear."

He waited some more. He waited while the notions of life and death chased each other across his mind until, at length, he realized that he didn't care that much about either of them anymore.

"What is that cost?"

"Nature must remain in balance. Everything within it is quintessentially in equilibrium. The cycles of life and death balance each other. Predators and their prey are in balance. Everything in nature evens out part of the whole. It is like this at all levels, the big and the small. Everything that exists helps to balance something else. And it is this ultimate harmony that allows life to continue.

"If anything in nature becomes out of sync, nature can readjust and, in time, regain its health. But when things are artificially thrown out of equilibrium, it is difficult for nature to recover.

"Nature is designed to regulate itself. When something operates outside of the principles of balance and a respect for them, then nature struggles to compensate for the error.

"Like when men cut down the trees of the jungle. Those trees are an important factor to the balance of the forest. They clean the air for all animals, including humans. They provide homes for animals and plants, and shade for those that cannot thrive in full sunlight. Their roots lend strength to the soil so that it does not erode in the rains. What the trees do for nature as a whole goes on and on.

"Many humans don't recognize the importance of balance. But I do. I know how significant it is. I understand it better than anyone else alive. And I know that if I were to save your life, there would be imbalance in the world. Life and death come when they are meant to. Conception and death are never accidents. Death arrives when you have fulfilled your purpose for this lifetime. Not before, and not after. Death is precise.

"One disruption to the equilibrium, even one so subtle as a whisper of the wind, is sufficient to endanger well-being. Sometimes, the imbalance does not end, but continues to cycle through nature, upsetting its harmony every time it passes."

He had waited all day to hear her explain why she couldn't save him. Yet now, he barely listened as she spoke. All he could think of was all the trees he had cut down before she took him away. He had thought so little of it then that he didn't even know how many trees he logged and dragged to a truck bed to be carted away.

"I was a logger. I cut down many trees. Why didn't you tell me this before?"

"Because once you were with me, you did not cut down trees anymore. You learned to respect life. There was nothing I needed to say then."

"But I could have gone back to the other loggers and told them about the need for balance in the rainforest. I could have helped them see that they should leave the trees alone."

"Do you really think you could have?"

He thought about it, unsure whether they would have listened. When he lived in Guayucuma, he viewed the forest as something to be subdued. The townspeople probably still did.

"There are humans that do not hear what they do not want to hear. Many are out of balance, and have been for a long time, for so long that they don't know how to attain equilibrium anymore. They have tried to remove themselves from nature in such a way as to see themselves separate from it and all its life.

"Humans have interfered with those elements in nature meant to balance it. There is little that can be done now except to let this imbalance run its course. Eventually, one day, its energy will fully dissipate and the opportunity to achieve harmony again will arrive."

"But I will not live to see it."

She shook her head. "No, you will not. But it is possible that neither will most humans."

"Yet you will?"

She nodded, back still straight, regal almost. "I will. I will be around until the very end."

"There will be an end for you too?"

"Yes. What is unknown is whether that end will come from balance or imbalance. And it will make a great difference at the end which of the two it is."

"Will you die then?"

"Yes, eventually, I will die. All life does."

"But you will not die soon."

"No."

"Are you really that different from me?" Even as he asked, it seemed an absurd question. Beauty radiated from her. She overflowed with life.

"In some ways, we are incredibly different. In others, we are not. Life is life, and the same essence courses through all of it. Richness, fullness, existence—it is within me as it is in you. I have told you before. You are man. I am mother."

He had asked her years before, *Whom was she mother to?* But he didn't think he'd understood her answer. He wasn't certain now that he had understood any of her answers, not truly.

"Whose mother are you?"

Then she smiled the first true smile of the day. It brimmed with the pride and joy common to all mothers. "I am mother to everyone and everything, even you."

He found that difficult to comprehend. He didn't know if perhaps his mind were too old and frayed to figure out what she was telling him. The key to understanding must be there, hiding from him in plain sight. Still, he didn't know if he would find it before death took him.

"I am woman. You are man. It is the quintessential essence of all creation. The feminine and the masculine, joined, create life."

He didn't grasp much of anything anymore, just that he knew how much he would miss life with her.

He didn't decide to, but he closed his eyes anyway. After a minute, he heard her stand. He didn't open his eyes to watch her elegantly unfold long legs and stand with firm muscles, her breasts and hair swaying slightly from the movement.

He must be about to die. He had never intentionally missed watching her. The beauty of her captivated him and was worth every moment he devoted to filling his memory with her.

Her hands were on him, caressing his long, gray hair and the white hairs that scattered across his chest. Again, she rested her hand on his heart. Was it to make sure it didn't break all over again with what she had to say next?

"Come on. Let's go. We have one last walk to share together."

She helped him stand while he tried not to cry. It didn't occur to him to look back at the home they had made to hold so many wonderful memories. He didn't fully comprehend the fact that he wouldn't return, that it was impossible to return to their home to live out what little was left of his life knowing she wouldn't be there to share it with him.

CHAPTER FOURTEEN

The Unwinding of the Last Bend

THE woman led him much as she had at the beginning, when he first traded his version of civilization for hers. She took his hand, smaller and frailer than
hers now, and walked next to him. Soon enough, he
would realize where she was taking him.

He didn't fear the rainforest's animals and plants anymore. He understood them, much like she did. He
knew the rolling levels of the forest ground, with its
heavy protruding roots and twisting vines, by memory.

She led him because she wanted to, because it would
be the last time.

They walked in the silent companionship that was so
common to them. Today, their silence was substantial;
within it fluttered all that could be said, but was not.
None of it mattered.

The man still didn't understand much, but it was possible that he never would before the final breath escaped his body. Even given an eternity of chances, he might not comprehend all the implications of what she had told him. In this life that was unwinding its last bend, unfolding before its great final disappearing act, he still knew more about limitations than freedoms, even with the life he had led in the jungle with this woman.

The woman understood everything that he did not. But there were certain things that words weren't meant to convey, and most of what the woman knew were these kinds of things.

The man would die with limited understanding, and both the man and the woman would accept this. It was within their natures, within who and what they were.

Walking with her, with his great love, the man didn't tire as much as he thought he would. He made it to the waterfall almost as easily as he used to, before age voiced its final say over his body.

Every time they arrived at the waterfall, it was as if it were the first. The water roared and frothed with undeniable power. When the man stood still, or even if he moved, he could sense the power of all of nature funneled into that one ferocious roar. The water was king of the jungle, pummeling anything in its path while it raced to plummet deep within the earth.

The Amazon River flowed lazily toward this spot, where it opened into a wide circle. And then the water had no choice but to crash to the rock bottom hundreds of feet below. That was its nature, and it transformed a circle of life temporarily into a circle of death.

The woman took a firmer grip on his hand and showed him to their place by the waterfall. It was the place to which they always came. She walked more slowly than usual while she waited for him to duck under the rock overhang and take steady steps across the moss-covered stone to the back of the shallow cave. It took longer for him to crouch down to the stone, but once he did, he sat in the same spot he had chosen since the beginning. He allowed his head to curve backward and lay on the rock; it cradled his neck with comfortable familiarity.

The man would miss everything about his life in the jungle with her. He would miss more than just her. He would miss all of it, the abundant life and variety that had become as much a part of him as he thought it could.

She squeezed his hand. She hadn't let go of it. She didn't want to let go of it ever again.

Yet she knew that she had to. That was why she'd brought him here.

They never spoke when they sat behind the waterfall, watching the water plunge in front of them in great big, crystalline sheets. It was like magic to him. Water, divided into droplets, held little power. Yet when the droplets combined almost infinitely as they did here, their power rumbled through him, vibrating all the way to his old aching bones.

The man didn't expect anything more than their usual routine, even though he knew today was different. She had said so.

He allowed himself to relax. He had learned long ago that it was futile to resist the water of this land. It was everywhere. It was meant to be everywhere, and it would be there long after he was gone.

He closed his eyes and didn't open them at the surprise of hearing her voice, powerful over the deafening pounding of the water. He didn't know how it was possible, but his lover's voice rose above the water easily. He heard no strain in it. It was as if she were whispering to him, impervious to the obstacles of earthly life.

He still didn't realize the obvious. That which was not hidden was hardest for him to see. It was within the wilds of the farthest reaches of the imagination, within the swirling rush of madness where the water finally plunged down to meet its horizon, where the possibilities of real truth could be grasped. Sometimes, the reality of impossibility lay beyond madness and beyond thought.

"I have loved you always. And I will love you again." Her voice trailed across the tired features of his face as if they were the slithering caresses of a newborn snake. He smiled. He had to. If these were indeed some of his last moments, then he would let the world know that he enjoyed them.

She scooted closer to him so as to leave no space between them. Skin pressed against skin, leaving no visible barrier. Brown against brown. Their long hair tangled together, intertwining, black and gray melding, different shades of the same color. Browns, blacks, grays, these were the colors of the earth. He opened his eyes to see how plain it was to him then: He was from the earth. He could see it; he was made up of the rich dirt and tree bark of his home.

"I will love you always." He spoke with the power left to him; it wasn't enough to rise above the thunderous claps of water. An ordinary person could not have heard his words, no matter how close his lips were to her ears. But she was not an ordinary person. So he continued, while the tears he thought he might not shed proved otherwise. "All the life within me is bound to you. You will always have my love, wherever I might go after I leave this body behind."

Even then, he didn't realize how deep the truth of his words ran. *All the life within me is bound to you.*

She nodded her confirmation. He didn't see it. He didn't need to.

"You are more handsome this time than you were the last." She raised her hand to draw it down the side of his face. This part was always the most difficult for her. She thought perhaps it would get easier next time, but it never did. Her human heart wrenched to know she would never touch that skin again. She would touch different skin, not this one.

Each representation of life was unique and would never repeat itself, not exactly. She knew this better than anyone else. It was a source of motherly pride, a human trait, just like the love that tore at her heart.

He found the richness of her brown eyes. "Last time?"

"Yes. We have loved each other many times before."

Tears ran down his face. Perhaps they wanted to join the waterfall. No one could blame them, to want to be part of something greater.

He smiled big and broad. His old cheeks seemed to split open, shiny and wet, making his face seem younger than it was even as his skin creaked. "We have loved each other before?"

"Oh yes. We have loved each other so much, so very much. Have you not felt that?"

"Yes, I believe I have. I must have. The love I hold for you seems to be the love of more than one lifetime, it is so great."

He felt as if he could spiral into the depths of her eyes, all the way down, anticipating the great loss that was coming, so palpably that he could feel it, his heart aflutter despite itself. He couldn't imagine a time when he couldn't stare into these eyes, when they wouldn't be there to mirror his reflection.

"Will you find me again? When I come into another body?"

"Yes. Of course I will. I always do. I always find you. I sense the moment you are born. And from then on I watch you until you become a man, until you and I can become lovers and share life and love once more."

His heart settled some. Could he dare hope that he would see her again?

"Do I remember you?"

She shook her head. A hint of sorrow foreshadowed her answer. "You never do. We start over every time."

"Have there been many times?"

"Yes. I have loved different versions of you hundreds of times, since it was decided that man should come to earth. I have loved you since your creation. You are man. I am woman and mother. We are destined to be together. I will continue to find you until the end."

"I won't forget you. Not this time. I promise."

"That is a promise you cannot keep."

"There is no way I will forget you. How could I? You fill me. You are a part of me. You are me." He spoke with a renewed spark of vitality. He was as sure of this as he was of himself.

She ran a hand along the other side of his face. "You always say something like that. And you always forget me."

He didn't say anything for a long time. Neither did she. The waterfall said it all for them, roaring loudly enough for the both of them, sounding out his pain and frustration more theatrically than he could. He was too old for theatrics.

He felt the last of his life waning. He had numbered words left to speak.

He had come to a point in his life when many things became finite, only to allow him to open to the infinite that was ripe within him, ready to flower.

He realized too late that last words didn't matter much when he had led the life he had with this woman. He wouldn't have a chance to speak them anyway. Not like he thought he would.

But then, nothing was like he thought it would be. It hadn't been for a very long time, if it had ever been at all.

CHAPTER FIFTEEN

The Unthinkable

THE woman had intended to finish it here, this human entanglement she insisted on diving into every time. Then, at the last moment, she feared the man would fall on the slippery stones if she left him there, alone with his inevitable sorrow. Death was coming for him soon, but she must allow death the opportunity to take his body as it meant to and not to have to salvage it from the pits of turmoil beneath the waterfall.

She helped him up without a word, and supported his arm while he stepped carefully. The roar of the water was enough to endanger his precarious stability.

She held him tightly. She was not about to watch him die now. She could not. She learned that hundreds of years before. Watching him die was no longer an option for her. Had her heart been able to break, watching him die would have broken it.

It had to be this way. She had to leave him. It was how she had done it since that one horrible time.

She could not be with him when he died. She had to be far away from the temptations that resulted from knowing she had the power to save him. It was something she would not allow herself to do, so why deal with the torment that came from understanding that the possibility still existed, intertwined with his last, rasping breaths?

They didn't have far to travel for him to be safe. At least, he would be safe enough. She always worried of what he would do once he watched her go. But that was his choice. It was always his choice. Despite who she was and who he was, she had never taken any of his choices away from him. She wouldn't start now.

They stood in familiar togetherness at the edge of the waterfall, at the edge of that great, thunderous bowl. There, the rocks were dry. She turned her back to the water and took both his hands. Even with the white, foaming water rushing behind her as a backdrop, his eyes focused easily on her. She was the most important thing to him. She had been even before he met her.

She looked into his eyes with an intensity that brought on immediate panic in him. She hadn't yet said a word. But it was written all over her face. She intended to leave him now.

All at once, his breathing grew rapid and he gripped her hands with all the strength left to his old body. He tried to pull her toward him as he had so many times before.

This time she didn't budge. She was decided and resigned. There was no sense in prolonging the inescapable.

She knew he thought there was more they needed to resolve first. But she also knew it would never be enough. They would never be ready for the finality of her next step and of his that would follow soon after.

By sunset that evening, death would come and go from this part of the jungle. He had only hours left. She knew exactly what color the sky would hold when breath rose from his body for the final time.

The color would be resplendent. Orange and red and violet, bright and brilliant, just as if it were his light on its journey home, moving toward the sun, a ball of flame that purified everything, even the intangibility of human life.

He wouldn't have long to mourn her, and he would need that time to settle himself for his transition. The passage from life into death was one meant to be traveled alone. It was the only way. Not even she could hold his hand from one to the next. She had tried and failed before.

She had tested so many different ways with him. There had been so many chances, so many lives. But after all her trying, it all came back to this.

His eyes jumped with useless movements. His eyeballs shook, looking for a way out of what he felt she was about to do.

She was about to walk off into the jungle. He already knew that if she left him and didn't want to be found, he would never find her, especially not now that he was old, but not even in his youth. She was the more powerful of the two.

Still, at the threshold of death, he didn't realize how powerful she was.

He stared into her eyes one final time, taking in all the depth of that warm, rich brown. And he did not see all there was to see. He looked into her eyes, not yet knowing who she was.

She expected this, though a small sliver of hope always existed, wondering if perhaps this lifetime he would recognize her for who she was.

He cracked his lips to speak some closing words—it was possible that any words would do, anything to forestall the inevitable. His parted lips trembled.

Desperation and loss froze him in place. They rooted him to the ground while he clung desperately to her hands.

She breached the contact between them. All the flesh he touched was that of fingers and palms. He wanted more. He yearned for more, for all that he had before, for all that he knew she couldn't give him anymore.

He thought to speak again, but this time she shook her head.

There was no need for any more words, for any more anything. The moment had arrived.

For the first time that he could remember, he resisted her guidance. He tried to pull her toward him and speak all at once.

As it turned out, that was the fateful impulse that precipitated her actions instead of delaying them as he'd hoped.

She twisted from him and pulled her hands from his grasp. In seconds, his hands held onto nothing, made all the more unbearable by what they had held instants before.

Horrified, transfixed, he watched as the woman he loved more than life walked toward the edge of the waterfall. She stopped a few feet from the actual drop-off to turn to look at him again. Even he knew what that look meant, but he couldn't accept what she was about to do.

She had said she would leave him to die alone. She was supposed to walk away. If she wanted, she could walk away without looking back.

But she could not die. He could not allow it. He was very certain it would kill him too if he had to watch what he now realized might happen. Her death would kill him.

He stepped toward her. Her eyes trailed to his feet, and he knew he had done it.

He had pushed her over the edge. She would jump before he could reach her.

With a radiant smile that would haunt him until sunset and death, she turned away from him and tilted her face to the sun. It beamed upon her. She seemed to glow with the richness the sun bestowed upon her, but which, truly, she already possessed.

Then she did the unthinkable.

The man ran to the precipice, clutching at his chest.

CHAPTER SIXTEEN

The Face of
the Infinite

THE man slipped at the edge, and almost fell. But he did not. Instead, he made it there in time to watch the woman dive into the heart of the waterfall with the same grace she revealed when she dove into his. Her arms trailed next to her body. Her feet pointed up; her head pointed down. She was only going one direction with that straight body, poised in purposeful flight.

He didn't breathe while he considered joining her. How easy it would be to jump off the edge as she had.

He watched as the brown body and black hair, small from his high perspective, vanished entirely. The froth foamed particularly violently, rising to meet her, to swallow her, greedily, hungrily.

Then she was gone.

He gulped for air. He clawed at his throat, at his chest, at the air, but nothing could dissipate the agony that ripped him apart.

It just was, simply, as it had to be.

There was no way around it. Nothing and no one would come to his aid. Destiny or the cycle of life—whatever it was—would fully unfold as it had to. Everything within nature knew not to interfere. Just as the woman had known not to interfere with the cycle of his life.

The preservation of balance was of the utmost importance. He didn't understand that then, and he didn't care to. What he wanted was to fling it all to hell.

He looked on at the frothing water incapable of shedding tears from the shock. This could not be happening. He refused to allow this to be the way it ended. He couldn't accept it. He would not.

How could she have died for him? It was so unfair. She had talked of the balance and how they couldn't upset it, but he couldn't imagine a greater transgression to nature's balance than to remove someone so full of life as her from it.

This was not right. It couldn't be. He stared down into the foam looking for her to pop up to catch her breath. It would be easy to spot her amid the white.

Yet even as he searched for signs of her, for a splash of brown skin or a strand of black hair, he knew her survival was an impossibility. No one could survive that drop, not even her. And less still could anyone survive the pounding that the water drummed on anything that fell into that pool. Her body could not withstand the pounding fists of angry giants. Even if they were made of water, they lacked all the gentleness of the single droplet.

He never did find the signs of the body that he searched for. But he did see something else, and that something brought him to his knees. His old knees landed on rough rock, and he didn't even notice.

A new kind of emotion trembled through him. If he had to name it, he would name it Elation, but he didn't know if even that was it. Perhaps the word for what he felt hadn't been coined yet.

There, far below, his beloved had survived the furious pounding of giants.

She had revealed that she was one of them.

He laughed at how many times she had told him who she was—no, what she was—and how many routes he had taken to dismiss this truth.

As incredible and impossible as it was, it was also undeniable. This truth she had tried to share with him before was indisputable now, reflected in everything that surrounded him. He could even feel it thumping with every beat of his heart, filling him when he thought nothing could ever fill him again.

She hadn't left him the way he thought she would, and it went far beyond her jumping into a waterfall when he thought she would walk away instead. She hadn't left him at all, not really.

He looked down at the plunging water, and there he found her smile. It radiated and shone from the white of the water, stronger than the sun. He heard her laughter echoing throughout the tree canopies, carried on the songs of birds. He saw her vitality reflected in the colors of the forest, and he discovered the rich brown of her eyes everywhere he looked for it.

He found her love still in his heart, right where it used to be, but now it was his to keep—until the sunset at least, until the next life.

She was everywhere. She was a part of all life.

Finally, he understood.

A fresh wave of tears was born from that understanding. So much went into those tears, not the least of which was regret for every tree he had cut down. Because now he saw that she was the tree. She was the singing bird and the slithering snake and the vibrant flower and the croaking frog with its suctioning feet. She was the jute and the snail and the ant, the worm and the moss and the water. She was the stone that lent him its strength. She was the air that lifted his spirits.

She had said it all along. He was man. She was woman. She was mother. It just hadn't occurred to him that she could be mother to it all.

But he saw it now. He saw her reflected in every thing that lived around him. He felt her inside him more than he had ever been inside her.

She did not die. She could not die. At least, she couldn't die like that, not at the bottom of a waterfall. When the end came for her, it would be a death worthy of someone—something—like her. She would explode in a deafening, blinding, numbing vision of light and color and sound so loud that it would thunder across the universe.

He could welcome death with open arms.

In the face of the infinite, death was nothing.

ABOUT THE AUTHOR

Lucía Ashta grew up in Argentina, and now lives among the red rocks of Sedona. She earned a degree in architecture from the University of Notre Dame, traveled the world, and became an attorney, before experiencing a spiritual awakening that changed the course of her life. Lucía has always written, and now dedicates herself to creating provocative stories that speak to the heart. Her books inspire you to believe in yourself, in the power of love and magic, and remain with you long after you put them down.

You can discover more about her and her work at
www.luciaashta.com.